VIVIAN AND THE LEGEND OF THE Hoodoos

BY TERRY CATASÚS JENNINGS

WITH GLENN ROGERS AND CLARENCE JOHN OF THE
SHIVWITS BAND OF THE PAIUTE INDIAN TRIBE OF UTAH

ILLUSTRATED BY PHYLLIS SAROFF

The rabbit brush was done blooming; pine nuts were ready for picking. Every year, groups from Vivian's Paiute band climbed the mesa to harvest them for winter. Vivian always helped Grandma. But today she had begged to come early, before anyone else. Basketball tryouts were in three hours.

"We'd better leave enough for the others," Grandma said. "You know what will happen if we don't."

"Yeah, yeah." Vivian smiled. "I know what will happen."

Vivian had memorized the legend. Long, long ago, the Old Ones, the *To-when-an-ung-wa*, had been bad. Most of the time, Grandma didn't say what they had done. But sometimes she said they had been greedy. They drank all the water from the rivers and streams. They even drank the snow melt in the spring. Nothing was left for other creatures to drink. When the pine nuts ripened, the *To-when-an-ung-wa* took them too. It wasn't long before the other creatures asked the god Sinawav the coyote for help.

Sinawav, who was a trickster, invited the old ones
to a huge banquet. He promised them all the food
they could eat and all the water they could drink.
The *To-when-an-ung-wa* were excited. When the
day finally came, they arrived at the feast dressed in
their best. But they never left.

When they were all together, the coyote punished them by turning them to rocky hoodoos. Now on moonlit nights, their spirits could be seen—shimmery shadows at the feet of the columns made from rock.

When Vivian was little, Grandma would say *hoooo-doooo*, drawing out the word. Scary, like an owl in the dark. That would always make Vivian obey.

Now Vivian was older. She knew erosion formed the hoodoo rocks, not a trickster spirit. Grandma knew that too. Still, whenever they saw a hoodoo, they teased each other. "Must have been bad," they said.

When they reached the piñon grove, Grandma wanted Vivian to ask the trees' permission to pick their fruits. Vivian was impatient.

"Come on," she said. "I already asked permission last year."

"Hrmph," Grandma said. She wasn't happy with Vivian. She asked the trees' permission herself. They got to work.

Grandma picked the low pine cones from one tree. Vivian shook the top branches with a tall stick to loosen the high ones.

Soon, Vivian started shooting pine cones into her bucket like basketballs. Two pointers, three pointers. Flip around the back and shoot.

"Didn't I teach you respect for every thing and every creature?" Now Grandma was really mad. She put down her basket and grabbed Vivian's hand.

"Come," she said.

"But I have basketball," Vivian complained.

"Come," Grandma said again.

Vivian had visited sites where the Old Ones had lived, other times, in other places. This one was different.

As she reached the clearing she almost stepped on a beautiful pottery sherd. White zigzags decorated a black background. She had to pick it up. It was bright, like the pot had broken just the day before.

Grandma took the pottery sherd from Vivian's hand and gently put it back.

"Things from long ago are sacred," Grandma said. "You shouldn't remove them."

Then the old woman took Vivian's face in her hand. "Our legends say we have always been here. Ten, fifteen people on this site. Ten, fifteen on other mesas north of here and east of here. Other clearings, other groups. They lived on high plateaus during the warm months. During cool spells, they stayed in caves in the valleys to keep warm.

"Our people depend on the land. On the little water the rivers and streams give us. On the creatures that give their lives to feed us. On the trees that give their fruit so we won't starve. We depend on each other."

Grandma's voice, like a Paiute lullaby, filled Vivian. It brought those who had lived on that mesa to life. Through Grandma's story, she could almost see them.

Here, a woman sorted pine nuts, singing the pine nut song. Next to her, a young boy slowly dropped pine nuts for his mother to grind.

A hunter knapped obsidian into tiny arrow points by a rock. Next to him, strips of meat dried in the sun.

An older woman sewed skins
into a blanket by a fire.

Next to a tree, another hunter strung a bow with yucca strings.

"They had to respect the trees, the creatures, and the water, Vivi," Grandma said. "If they didn't, they would die."

Slowly, Grandma led her through the ruins. Chips of obsidian littered the ground by a rock. By the ruins of a pit house lay an awl made of bone, perfect for sewing skins. And close to the tree line, a smooth, slender blade of locust wood was barely covered by the sandy soil. It had a notch at one end. Once it had been a bow. Vivian knelt by a large stone and ran her hand over its surface. A gentle dip had been rubbed smooth in its center. It was a *metate* for grinding nuts and grains.

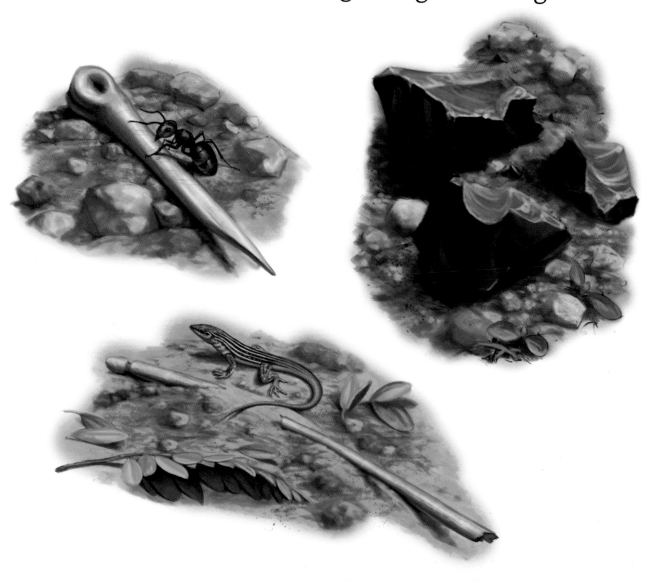

Vivian and Grandma returned to the piñon grove to finish their task. This time Vivian asked the trees' permission without being told. She filled her bucket many times, always with respect.

"Thank you. Thank you for giving your fruit so that we may live," she said when she left.

For Creative Minds

Paiute Culture and History

Native American Nations

The Paiute have lived in southwestern North America for a long time. Paiute legends say they have always been there. This area is now part of Utah, Arizona, Nevada and California.

The Paiute lived in the high desert. They stayed on mesas, plateaus, and mountains. They also lived in the river valleys between these plateaus.

Archeologists are scientists who study how people lived long ago. They have found arrow points in Paiute lands that are 10,000 years old. These likely came from the Paiute's ancestors. There are pithouses and pottery pieces from 2,000 years ago.

Altitude: height above sea-level

High desert: an area at high altitude with little rain

Mesa: a small plateau with steep sides

Plateau: a large area with a flat top and steep drop on at least one side

In this desert environment, the summers were hot, more than 100° F (38° C). The winters were well below freezing.

The Paiute traveled throughout the year to farm and hunt. But they didn't have far to go to follow their food sources. Instead of traveling long distances, they moved up and down. In the summers, they lived in wikiups high in the mountains where it was cool. In the winters, they lived in warm caves near the canyon floor. The Paiute take their name from this seasonal journey. Paiute means, "traveling back and forth" in their own language.

The Paiute relied on the plants and animals in the high desert. All year long, the Paiute hunted rabbits and quail with traps and on drives. At high altitudes, they hunted deer, desert big horn sheep, elk, and pronghorn antelope. They dried the meat for winter and used the skins for clothing and blankets. They ate beans of mesquite trees, wild rice, berries, prickly pear cactus, sage, squaw bush, and watercress. The Paiute grew corn and developed irrigation for their crops. They made shampoo from yucca root and used the sharp needles of the yucca leaves to sew. They made rope, moccasins, and bowstrings from the yucca fiber.

The Paiute picked pine nuts in the fall. They shelled, roasted, and ground them into flour. This flour was easy to carry and store through the winter. They used the flour to make cakes or paste. They could eat the pine-nut paste like oatmeal or make it into a drink like a protein shake.

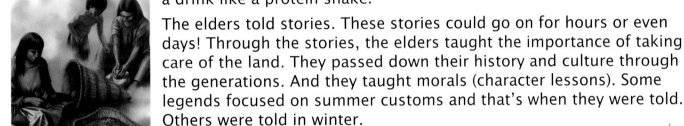

The elders told stories. These stories could go on for hours or even days! Through the stories, the elders taught the importance of taking care of the land. They passed down their history and culture through the generations. And they taught morals (character lessons). Some legends focused on summer customs and that's when they were told. Others were told in winter.

The legend of the hoodoos tells how the trickster god, Sinawav the coyote, turned the Old Ones into rocks. This story teaches that those who do wrong will be punished. It also explains the hoodoos, tall rocks created by erosion. Vivian's grandmother uses the word *hoodoo* to remind Vivian of the story and to get her to behave.

 Is there a word or a story that elders in your family use to get you to behave?

Vivian's people depended on their environment. The high desert only had enough food for a few people in an area. So the Paiute lived in small bands. Paiute bands always helped each other because they knew that someday they might need help too. They were a very welcoming and peaceful people. Families and individuals often visited other bands. They sometimes stayed for long periods before returning to their homes.

In the 1800s, American settlers came to the Paiute lands. The Paiutes welcomed the visitors as they did other Paiute bands. But the settlers never left. And they never gave back or helped the Paiute. Instead, they took over Paiute land and left the Paiute without resources.

Today there are five bands of the Paiute Indian Tribe of Utah (PITU): Cedar Band of Paiutes, Indian Peaks Band of Paiutes, Kanosh Band of Paiutes, Koosharem Band of Paiutes, and Shivwits Band of Paiutes. Most of the Paiute live on PITU Tribal Reservations in Utah. Their government is the Tribal Council. Each band has its own Band Council and sends a representative to the Tribal Council.

Water Shapes The Rock

Weathering and erosion change rocks and mountains. They change our earth.

Weathering breaks down rocks and minerals. There are two types of weathering: mechanical and chemical. Mechanical weathering is caused by water, ice, wind, and changes in temperature. These forces break off pieces of larger rocks. Chemical weathering is caused by water, carbon dioxide, and oxygen. They change the minerals in the rock into different, softer forms.

Erosion happens when water, wind and gravity move the weathered pieces away from the mother rock.

Weathering and erosion make many kinds of changes to the land. Rushing water carves ruts, ditches, washes, and canyons. It smooths out hollow places. Rushing water can come from floods, heavy rains, and melting snow. Dripping water seeps through a crack on a rock and carries away grains of sand. Dripping water can make caves, windows, or pockets. It can even make an arch.

Water fills cracks in the rock. When the temperature drops below freezing, water turns to ice. The ice expands in the crack. The crack becomes wider and deeper. When a crack is wide enough and deep enough, it causes a piece to separate from the mother rock. This process is called **ice wedging**.

Weathering and erosion shape the landscape.

Ice Wedging Experiment

For this experiment, you will need:
- flour
- water
- a mixing bowl and fork
- a balloon
- two disposable cups

Take the balloon and fill it with some water. It should be able to fit inside your cup, so don't overfill it. Tie the balloon off and set it aside.

In your bowl, mix three cups of flour with two cups of warm water. Stir with the fork until there are no lumps left.

Pour some of your flour mix into the bottom of one cup. Once the bottom is covered, place your balloon in the cup. Then add more mix to cover the balloon.

In your second cup, pour in your flour mix until it is level with the mix in the first cup.

Allow the flour mix to dry and harden completely.

After the mix is dry, place both cups in the freezer and leave them overnight.

What do you see when you take the cups out of the freezer the next morning? Has anything changed?

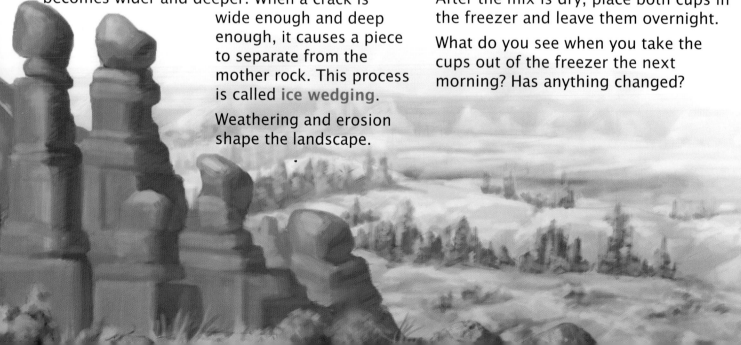

Hoodoos

A hoodoo is a tall, skinny column of rock. Hoodoos can be as small as a person or as tall as a building. Some hoodoos are taller than a ten story building (150 feet, 45 meters). Hoodoos and similar rock structures have many names—goblins, chimneys, columns, and spires. They are all formed in a similar way, by millions of years of weathering and erosion.

There are four stages in the making of a hoodoo. Put the following stages in order to unscramble the name of the modern Paiute tribe. The answer is below.

I When canyons run in roughly the same direction, they form **fins**—freestanding rock walls between the canyons. Water can collect in cracks (joints) across the fins. When water freezes and ice forms in the joints, the cracks expand.

T After many cycles of freezing and thawing (ice wedging), cracks in the fin become deeper and wider. Water can seep down the rock and create **windows**.

P A **plateau** is a high, flat landform. Rushing water weathers and erodes the plateau. This creates ruts and washes on the earth's surface. Over millions of years, the washes can deepen to canyons.

U Over time, the window collapses or the fin separates into individual spires. This leaves a freestanding column: a **hoodoo**. Hoodoos will continue to weather and erode. Eventually, the once-tall hoodoo will be a mound of soil.

The Colorado Plateau is a large landform that covers parts of Utah, Colorado, Arizona, and New Mexico.

Bryce Canyon is in a part of the Colorado Plateau that used to be Paiute territory. Soft limestone layers and more than 200 days of freeze-thaw cycles each year make this a perfect place for ice wedging and erosion. At Bryce Canyon, many hoodoos formed in a bowl-shaped basin. It looks like a sunken city of hoodoos. This is likely where the legend of the hoodoos originated.

Answer: PITU (Paiute Indian Tribe of Utah)

To Callen Wade Jennings who loves the hoodoos.—TCJ

To my student and model, Georgia.—PS

Thanks to Dr. Larry E. Davis, Education Outreach/Geologist at Bryce Canyon National Park for verifying the accuracy of the geology information in this book, and to Glenn Rogers and Clarence John of the Shivwits Band of the Paiute Indian Tribe of Utah for verifying the accuracy of the information regarding Paiute culture and history.

Library of Congress Cataloging-in-Publication Data

Names: Jennings, Terry Catasús, author. | Saroff, Phyllis V., illustrator.
Title: Vivian and the legend of the hoodoos / by Terry Catasús Jennings ; with Glenn Rogers and Clarence John of the Shivwits Band of the Paiute Indian Tribe of Utah ; illustrated by Phyllis Saroff.
Description: Mount Pleasant, SC : Arbordale Publishing, [2017] | Includes bibliographical references. | Summary: When Vivian is disrespectful to the trees and the land, Grandma relates the Paiute legend of the trickster god Sinawav the coyote who turned the bad Old Ones into stone columns. | Includes bibliographical references.
Identifiers: LCCN 2016043597 (print) | LCCN 2016049193 (ebook) | ISBN 9781628559576 (english hardcover) | ISBN 9781628559583 (english pbk.) | ISBN 9781628559590 (spanish pbk.) | ISBN 9781628559606 (English Downloadable eBook) | ISBN 9781628559620 (English Interactive Dual-Language eBook) | ISBN 9781628559613 (Spanish Downloadable eBook) | ISBN 9781628559637 (Spanish Interactive Dual-Language eBook)
Subjects: LCSH: Paiute Indians--Southwest, New--Fiction. | CYAC: Paiute Indians--Fiction. | Indians of North American--Southwest, New--Fiction. | Behavior--Fiction. | Grandmothers--Fiction.
Classification: LCC PZ7.J429879 Vi 2017 (print) | LCC PZ7.J429879 (ebook) | DDC [E]--dc23
LC record available at https://lccn.loc.gov/2016043597

Translated into Spanish: *Viviana y la leyenda de los Hoodoos*

Lexile® Level: AD 580

key phrases: character, chimneys (rock), column (rock), community, desert, erosion, fables/folktales, geography, geology, history, hoodoos, landforms, physical change, Paiute, spire, trickster, Utah, Native American

Bibliography:
Garfield County Tourism Bureau. Utah's Bryce Canyon Country. "Red Painted Faces - Native American Lore." Web. Accessed 02/05/15.
Hebner, William L. and Plyler, Michael. *Southern Paiute: A Portrait*. Logan, Utah: Utah State University Press, 2010. Print.
Knack, Martha C. *Boundaries Between: The Southern Paiutes, 1775-1995*. Lincoln, NE: University of Nebraska Press, 2001. Print.
Martineau, LaVan. *Southern Paiutes, Legends, Lore, Language and Lineage*. Las Vegas, NE: KC Publications, 1992. Print.
National Public Radio. "All Things Considered." "Listen to the Story." July 1, 2008. Web. Accessed 2/05/15.
U.S. Department of Interior. National Park Service, Bryce Canyon. *Geology of Bryce Canyon—Odyssey of an Oddity*. Leaflet.
U.S. Department of Interior. National Park Service, Bryce Canyon. Hoodoos. Web. Accessed 2/05/15.
Zion National-Park.com. Hikes in and Around Zion National Park. Web. Accessed 02/05/15.

Manufactured in China, December 2016
This product conforms to CPSIA 2008
First Printing

Arbordale Publishing
Mt. Pleasant, SC 29464
www.ArbordalePublishing.com